FORBIDDEN
MEMORIES

If you enjoy reading this book,
you might like to try another story
from the **MAMMOTH READ** series:

FORBIDDEN MEMORIES

Jamila Gavin

ILLUSTRATED BY
MARK ROBERTSON

mammoth

First published in Great Britain in 1998 by Mammoth
an imprint of Reed International Books Limited
Michelin House, 81 Fulham Road, London SW3 6RB

ISBN 0 7497 3074 9

10 9 8 7 6 5 4 3 2 1

A CIP catalogue record for this book is
available from the British Library

Printed in Great Britain by Cox & Wyman Ltd,
Reading, Berkshire

Contents

1 The secret

We were born as one, and one we
will remain.
Distance cannot break our bond,
nor time bring forgetfulness.
And when one ceases to exist, the
other will too.

THE TWINS WROTE their secret pledge together the day before they learned they were to be separated.

'We'll never forget each other,' Sasha whispered tearfully.

'Never, never,' Devi pledged, clasping her sister's hands.

'And we'll always be there for each other, in our heads? We'll mind-talk whenever we need to?'

'We will always have our secret communication.'

'They can't take that away from us, can they?' Sasha was always the fearful one.

'They can if we're careless and get found out. But we won't take risks. We can go into white out, blanking our brains so that nothing can penetrate.'

They spent their last day together, hand in hand, their sadness stripping them of any further words.

Even before they learned to speak, Devi and Sasha mind-talked. They could communicate with each other just by thinking, and they always knew what the other was feeling or doing.

Devi had taught Sasha. As they grew older, she would think up experiments to strengthen their power and to learn to

control it, and how they delighted in being able to joke, make up fantasies, share secrets – all without opening their mouths.

Their Dome parents became aware of it and warned the twins that telepathy was a criminal offence. But Devi and Sasha couldn't help it. It was like trying to prevent them using an arm or a leg.

The Dome controlled everything; it decided who should be born, how, when and with what genes. From the egg bank, the determiners selected future citizens for the different zones and fertilised them to be thinkers, artists, wealth creators and operators, adding or manipulating genes as necessary.

Ever since Sasha and Devi were reared

from one egg, the Dome had watched them carefully. They knew these twins were special. Both had been born with such extraordinary gifts that hardly any genetic interference was necessary. But the power of such gifts combined in the dual strength of these sisters was a threat to the security of the Dome, and the Dome determiners decided that the twins must be separated after childhood. Sasha would be a dancer and Devi a scientist.

Sasha was engineered with genes from the finest dancers that the world had ever known. But it was Devi who was considered the prize. She was the one in millions who was of natural, superintelligence, with a scientific brain as brilliant as Einstein or Curie or Faraday. She would be given star status in the Dome, and one day would be a Dome tutor. Until then, she would live in Science Sector A, under the instruction of the legendary Chief Tutor.

On the day of separation nothing could ease the pain. The Dome determiners declared their childhood over. Each twin was apprenticed to their special tutor in different parts of the Dome. They would never see each other except on Regeneration Day, every ten years. But no matter where they were and how far apart, Devi had made sure they would always be able to communicate.

'Never forget our pledge,' Sasha's grief was transmitted with her thoughts.

'Never, never!' came Devi's silent reply.

2 Regeneration Day

DEVI GLIDED ALONG the stainless steel corridor to the regeneration suite. She was happy. It was a special day. Not only was it Regeneration Day – the one day when she and her twin could meet face to face – but she and Sasha were a hundred years old.

'I can't wait to see you,' Sasha's voice came into her head.

'Me too!' replied Devi. 'I've got a great present for you. See you in the reception area.'

Devi's present was a video disc which she had compiled, containing images reflecting the whole of Sasha's life from early childhood, when they had lived together, to the glorious career Sasha had made as the greatest dancer of her time. She couldn't wait to give it to her.

Devi entered the reception area. It was packed with others who shared the same birth date, waiting patiently for their turn. They knew each other's faces, and greeted one another cheerily. Devi's eyes skimmed the room, eagerly looking for Sasha. Yes, there she was – there was no mistaking her long, willowy dancer's body. Sensing her sister's arrival, Sasha turned with a brilliant smile and waved. But before they could get across to each other, Devi heard her name being summoned. 'Will Devi, Cat A SS 2534 please report to the regeneration chamber.' They stopped, shrugged at each other and laughed. 'Oh well!'

'I'll see you back here afterwards,' Devi silently told her.

'I'll be waiting,' responded Sasha. 'Oh and, Devi,' she added, as her twin moved towards the regeneration chamber, 'Happy birthday.'

Devi nodded joyfully, 'Happy birthday,' and entered the chamber.

Regeneration was a full body and brain check-up, something all Category A people underwent for as long as the Dome had a use for them. This meant limb maintenance, skin rejuvenation, an organ check on heart, lungs, kidneys, liver and eyes in case they needed to be replaced, and an hour-long session in the brain capsule where the brain cells received an electrical boost.

'What have you been up to, Devi?' It was Roy – one of the more friendly robot mechanics. 'Your pulse is racing and your blood pressure's up. Is everything all right?'

Devi smiled and tried to look relaxed as she entered the softly lit examination room. Regeneration Day brought with it a certain anxiety. Regeneration wasn't automatic. Each person had to be a wealth creator or a positive contributor to the Dome, otherwise they were classified non-economic and 'decommissioned' – allowed to die. Also, the slightest alteration in physical or mental performance could result in decommissioning and, recently, in her sleep she had been seeing pictures, dreams; and dreams were forbidden because they were made of memories. She should have reported them, but her friend Gretel had been sent away for brain reprocessing after *she* had reported a dream. Gretel had emerged a totally different person. She was like one of the robot class. She didn't even recognise Devi.

'Everything's fine,' she told Roy. 'I'm just excited. I've got this great present for Sasha and I'm longing to give it to her.'

'Sounds good. Well, we'll soon have this over with.'

Other RMs were in attendance. Their insect-like bodies moved silently round the suite carrying out tests and collating

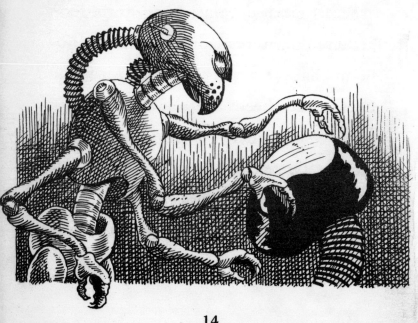

data on each person, which was fed into the physician computer. This analysed the information and printed out a diagnosis and prescription for treatment.

Roy brought up Devi's file on the screen. 'Hmm . . . you had visual and aural enhancement last time. Has it all worked well? They're guaranteed for fifty years.'

'Yes, I can see and hear up to factor fifteen. I think I'm fine.' She could feel the diagnostic ultrasound playing over her and the barely audible clickety clicking of the physician computer as it recorded all her details on to its database.

'Yup, looks like you're still good. Let's get you into capsule BB3 for the brain boost.'

Devi slid inside and allowed herself to be connected up to a series of terminals which were fitted to half a dozen different points on her head. She never liked this bit. It always hurt – though never for more than about five seconds.

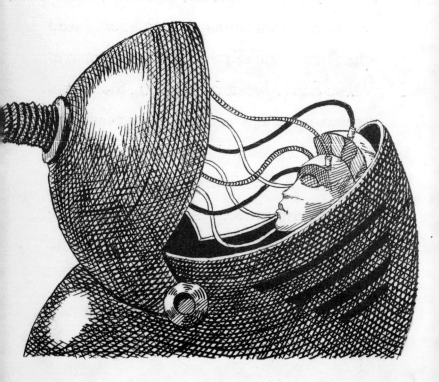

'Ready?' smiled Roy.

'Ready,' she smiled back.

Roy sealed her in, plunging her into a coffin-like darkness. Gradually, Devi felt the electrical current throbbing into her brain. Roy was increasing the charge. Gradually, gradually, stronger and stronger. Now. Stop now. Now! It had reached her threshold of pain. She felt a scream rising up her throat. It was usually over by now. It had never gone as far as this before. But it didn't stop. The pain went on and on increasing. And, with the pain, an extraordinary picture came into her head . . .

Devi began to scream.

3 Mind pictures

THE SCREAM SEEMED to go on for ever. Another voice had taken it up and extended the dreadful sound.

When Devi returned to the reception area after the brain boost, the scream still hung in the air, reverberating on and on. She immediately looked round for her sister. Where was she?

'Have you seen Sasha?' she asked the other dancers.

'She had an upset,' someone told her. 'A pain in her head. She was screaming.

They're doing her in the X shift.'

Suddenly Sasha emerged from the regeneration chamber, flanked by two robot escorts. Devi felt fear sweep over

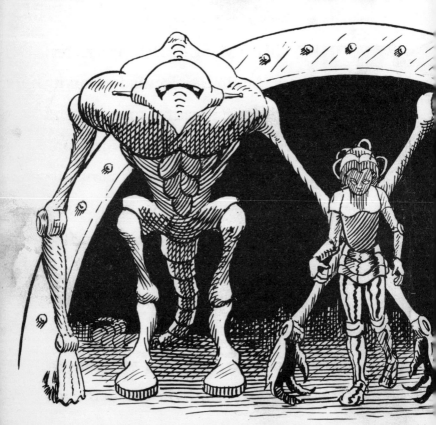

her. The escorts meant she was under suspicion. Desperately, she tried to catch Sasha's attention, but Sasha kept her eyes to the floor, her mind in defensive mode – a blank white-out.

Devi focused every ohm of her electrical activity into Sasha's head. 'Come on, Sasha! Come on. Look up!'

At last, Sasha looked up, startled as if suddenly awoken. Her face was distorted with fear. Briefly they caught each

other's gaze, but there was no under-
standing. Sasha was led away and never
looked up again.

'Raan!'

'Mmm?'

'Something funny happened to me in
the regeneration capsule.' Devi spoke from
her sleep pad in the rest bay. She had to
tell someone and Raan was her best
friend.

'What?' Raan had been on the brink of
sleep and was annoyed at being disturbed.

'I don't know for sure. I think there
may have been an electrical disturbance
– a short circuit or something. I thought
my brain was going to burst. It was

terrible. I was yelling to be let out, but those RMs didn't notice anything – the dumb idiots.'

'You should have pressed the alarm button.'

'I did. Nothing happened. Something went wrong in the capsule, I know it did. The RMs said I was mistaken because it didn't show up on the computer.'

'They're probably just looking out for their own skins. They know they would be decommissioned for negligence if any-thing went wrong.'

'By the time I got out, Sasha was gone. And then . . .' she began to sob quietly.

'You OK?' Raan's voice was soft with concern.

'Sort of . . .' Devi stared tearfully into the darkness, wondering how much she should tell. Something was terribly wrong. All she could think about was Sasha. She must have seen what Devi saw during her brain boost – and now they had caught Sasha.

The brain scanner cruised around the rest bay. A beam of light swept over the sleeping heads, ready to pick up on any forbidden brain activity. Devi lay still and created a white out in her head. The brain scanner moved on.

When she was sure she would be undisturbed, Devi concentrated hard, activating the telepathic part of her brain. 'Come on, Sasha, speak to me, speak to me!' In the silence, her breathing was so faint that she was almost comatose.

'Devi. It's me, Sasha.'

Like a single, soft note, Sasha's voice slid into her head. 'I'm sorry I couldn't contact you sooner. They drugged me. This is goodbye. They're coming for me soon, Devi. I saw your mind picture on

Regeneration Day. It hurt and I screamed, but it was wonderful. It just swept into my head. I wanted to ask you about it, but the brain scanner picked it up . . . Oh, Devi, be careful. Remember Gretel. Whatever you do, don't dream.'

Devi was filled with dread. 'Sasha! It's my fault. I taught you to make your brain into a receiver. I didn't mean this to happen. What are they going to do? Who is coming for you? Where are they taking you?'

'The Dome Court. I'm up before the Committee. They will decide whether to reprocess me or decommission me. Devi. Remember our pledge? I'll always . . .'

The message stopped short. Devi sat up

violently like a sleep walker harshly awakened. 'Sasha!' she called out into the night.

The brain scanner halted and turned rapidly, focusing its beam on her. Devi bowed her head over her knees and sadly slipped into white out.

'Are you sure you're OK?' Raan's voice was full of concern.

She waited until the brain scanner finally moved on. 'Yes. Just disturbed sleep patterns. I miss my sister, that's all. You know how much she means to me. I suppose it will be another ten years before I see her . . . and all because of a stupid fault . . . It gave me an awful headache . . . I blacked out I think and . . .'

'And what?' Raan leaned up on one elbow.

'Well I saw, a sort of . . . picture. Ever since then I've been seeing more mind pictures. Honestly, Raan, they are extraordinary. Have you ever experienced anything like it?'

'What sort of pictures?' Raan asked guardedly.

Devi bit her lip fiercely. She mustn't say any more. It was too dangerous. 'They aren't exactly pictures . . .' she back-tracked. 'More feelings . . . yes, odd sorts of feelings. I'm sure it was to do with that extra dose of electricity they gave me. It was bound to have an effect.' She paused. 'Don't think about it any more, Raan.'

She listened in darkness, wondering if he believed her. She yawned loudly, then said in a deliberately sleepy voice, 'Goodnight, Raan.'

'Goodnight, Devi.'

For a long time into the night, Devi lay awake. She was full of terror for Sasha, but she was also bursting with curiosity. Mind pictures. Was she mad? She felt on the brink of discovery.

'I have been something else before.'

4 The Chief Tutor

THE CHIEF TUTOR was eight hundred years old. Living for ever had been part of the deal. He sighed. It had seemed a good bargain at the time – his genius and skills in exchange for everlasting life or, at least, life for as long as he wanted it. He would have decommissioned himself a long time ago if they hadn't begged him not to – in fact, ordered him not to. Despite all the skills of genetic engineering they had not, until now, managed to produce another being of equal genius to himself, so he was forced to go on living.

Then Devi was created. The Tutor was flabbergasted, amazed but, above all, overjoyed. Devi was the person for whom he had been waiting for three hundred years. Someone who could take his place.

Over the next decades, the Tutor instructed her in all the disciplines of mathematics, physics, quantum mechanics and cosmology. He developed her brain, trained her memory, activated all sections of her mind.

But he had to be careful. There was one area of the brain which was automatically removed in almost all Dome citizens of every category: the zone of inherited

33

memory and imagination; the danger area where mind pictures were produced which could lead to the authority of the Dome being challenged and undermined. The Chief Tutor made the case on Devi's behalf, arguing that she was too rare a genius to tamper with any part of her brain. The Dome determiners agreed, on condition that if she ever revived that part of her brain, she would be reprocessed.

Until now, it hadn't mattered; it need never have mattered, if only Devi hadn't ever asked the question he had always dreaded.

It came at the end of the day when they had worked intensively for hours. Devi pushed herself away from her computer. Her face was pale and it was as if she had been holding her breath for a long time. 'Why . . .?' she paused.

'Yes,' he said encouragingly. 'Have you a question for me? I hope I can answer it – they have been getting rather complicated these days.' He smiled.

'Why . . . why is it wrong to see pictures in your head?'

The Tutor stopped smiling. There was a long silence.

'Does it mean that I'm breaking down?' she asked quietly, sensing his unease.

'What have you seen?' He tried to sound casual, but a deep chasm of despair began to open up inside him.

'I have seen a wide, grey arc. I have seen a great shining surface – not still, but constantly moving and changing colour. There is a high, white wall – at least, I think it's a wall; yet it is curved like the grey arc and pitted with holes. Things fly in and out of the holes. What is it? Is it a place? Does it exist?'

'I wondered if the day would come when you would see the pictures,' murmured the Tutor. 'I was afraid someone else would find out before me. It is forbidden. You know the penalty could be decommissioning.'

'Yes,' she said simply.

'How long, Devi? How long has this been going on?'

'Since my last brain boost. I think there was a fault – and, unfortunately . . .' She stopped. Now was the danger. Now was the moment when she put her life and Sasha's into the hands of her tutor. '. . . I communicate telepathically with Sasha – that's how we've always kept in touch – and she saw my picture. It was my fault.'

'I see,' he said softly and closed his eyes.

'I know telepathy is wrong, but we've never harmed anyone. It was our way of being together. No one knows how awful it was for us to be separated. And it's my fault she saw the pictures.'

The Tutor leaned back with his eyes still closed. Devi wondered if he had fallen asleep.

'Please tell me where she is.'

The Tutor didn't speak.

'What did they do to her? Why were we not able to meet on our last Regeneration Day? Has Sasha been decommissioned?'

At last the Tutor opened his eyes. 'She has not been decommissioned, I can tell you that,' he said quietly. 'She has been given a trial period. She is to be reprocessed.'

'Can I see her?'

'I can't tell you where she is or give you any reasons. It would be dangerous. This conversation is already dangerous. If the Dome finds out, even I couldn't help you. I don't want to lose you. It mustn't happen, it must not happen,' the Tutor repeated with quiet vehemence.

'What she saw was my fault. It is not she who should be reprocessed, but me!' Devi cried desperately. 'I see pictures all the time now. They look familiar yet unknown to me. What does it mean?'

'It means,' said the Tutor carefully, 'that you are remembering your origins. You have revived genetic memory built into your DNA, inherited from your ancestors from generations back.'

Devi felt a surge of excitement, almost as painful as the extra boost of electricity which had triggered her memory.

'We are the original human beings who were brought into the safe haven to preserve the human race,' the Tutor explained. 'Almost a thousand years ago, most of the planet was laid waste through nuclear wars, pollution, drought and deforestation. Global warming had caused huge amounts of land to disappear under the sea. What land was left was barely able to sustain life. Most of the world's species were made extinct and the human race itself was about to die out. We created this Dome, a safe haven for a small number of chosen people. We banned mind pictures because they reminded people of the outside world and brought back all their old hatreds and prejudices. Dreams are the kaleidoscope of our memories. We couldn't allow them in the Dome.'

Devi listened – and it was as if all those strange feelings were suddenly explained.

'Devil!' the Tutor's voice interrupted her thoughts. 'Let Sasha go. There's nothing you can do for her now – and we need you. I need you. You must not tell any one

about your mind pictures. I will control that. I shall organise treatment which will help you to forget her, and soon there will be no reason to ever discuss this again.'

No, no! Devi cried inwardly. Never make me forget my sister. I will never forget.

'Devi?'

'Can I ask one last thing?'

The Tutor leaned back and closed his eyes. 'Ask it,' he said with a sigh.

'Is the outside world completely dead?'

The pause stretched on and on.

'Yes. Yes!' The Tutor had never seemed more old. 'Completely dead. There is no other world but the Dome.'

5 Finding Sasha

'D^{EVI!}'

'What?' Devi tried to sound on the brink of sleep.

'Have you seen any more pictures in your head?'

Devi was silent for a brief second. She hated lying to Raan.

'No,' she lied.

'I wouldn't report you, Devi. You're my best friend.'

Devi was silent. Every night she

dreamed. Controlled dreams; maintaining a half sleep so that she could blot them out if necessary. Pictures flowed into her head. Faces peered out at her – half remembered. Who were they? What were they doing in her head? Sometimes they smiled at her and she would wake fully, sitting up in the darkness, clamping shut her mouth so that she didn't shout out, 'Who are you?' And always there was the grey arc; the shining, moving surface and the high, white wall with things which flew in and out. Could the Tutor be wrong? Could there be a life outside the Dome?

'You're my best friend too, Raan,' she murmured sadly.

The brain scanner came by. It stopped

a little longer in front of Devi. Probably the Tutor had programmed it to scan her more closely just to ensure that his therapy had worked. Devi had invoked white out, but felt a twinge of anxiety that the scanner would pick up something. It moved on.

'Oh, Raan, I want to find Sasha. She's been reprocessed. I know she may not recognise me if I ever meet her again, but I must find her.'

'Then let me help you,' whispered Raan. 'I can hack into the main frame computer. I can help you to surf the Web sites. It will be quicker if we both do it.'

'It's dangerous. If we were found out . . .'

'It's dangerous, but I want to help you.'

So, in the days that followed, Raan and Devi began hacking. Like ancient explorers, they probed restlessly, roaming from one Web site to another. They extended the search, moving deeper and deeper into the secrets of the Dome,

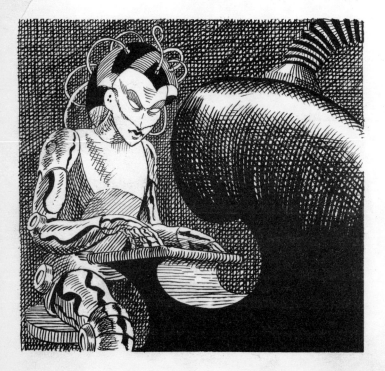

hacking into libraries, ancient archives and the confidential files.

One night alone, just when her eyes were closing with fatigue, Devi hit a button – she hardly knew which one – and there it was. The name gleamed on the screen:

Sasha Cat S 2234
Recommissioned to
Sector D, clone sector,
for trial reprocessing

Devi burst into tears. At least Sasha was still alive, but for how long? They must leave the Dome. Devi hacked into the cartography section and plotted the route which led out of the Dome.

Now she had to rescue Sasha.

She didn't tell Raan of her discovery. She was already responsible for Sasha's fate and she didn't want to risk Raan as well. She told him she had stopped looking.

Raan was puzzled. 'You can't give up! It's not like you, Devi. Let me . . .'

'No, Raan, no more. She has already been decommissioned.' She tried to speak gently. 'Leave it. Don't look any more. It's too dangerous for you. But thank you. I'll never forget what a good friend you've been.' She tried not to see the hurt in his eyes.

★   ★   ★

Devi took the descent car down, down, down to the very core of the Dome where glass, steel and plastic gave way to earth and rock. She told the robot guardian that she was researching ancient rock stratification. She knew it sounded convincing, and she was certain he would be ignorant of the fact that at the bottom of the shaft was a secret passage which led straight to Sector D.

The Dome rules stated that a robot guardian should stay with her at all times, but this robot knew Devi, and he was relieved when she said that she could manage on her own. So Devi descended alone.

Down at the lowest stratum of the Dome,

under the ever-roaming eye of the electronic camera, Devi pretended to examine layers of rock, making notes on her computer. Her work looked repetitive and boring. No one could watch her with undivided attention for long. After a while, she edged her way casually towards what looked like a small cave. This was the entrance to a passageway leading to Sector D.

Her body was not designed for such rough terrain and she had to proceed carefully. She passed through strange regions where stalagmites and stalactites had hung and risen for millions of years; she edged her way round terrifying deep, green pools – knowing that if she fell in she would never be able to get out. There was only the light from her torch to guide her. Sometimes it seemed too feeble to illuminate the pitch black tunnels, yet other times it caught the clusters of crystal, which flared like chandeliers, lighting up the caves as bright as day.

The ground beneath her feet was full of pits and gullies. It was rocky and uneven, raw and primeval – something she had never seen in the upper regions of the Dome. It slowed her down, for if she damaged any part of her limb structure, she would be beyond help.

Bit by bit, with the help of her map, she reached the far exit which led into Sector D.

'Sasha!' She kept trying to make contact. 'Sasha! Speak to me. Please.' But nothing came through – not even the slightest quiver of communication. Full of foreboding, Devi found the door to Sector D and opened it.

A great space stretched and expanded upwards and outwards. Lifts fell and rose like bubbles in test tubes; escalators ascended and descended carrying more and more workers from one level to another. It was teeming with clones performing all sorts of different tasks: compiling spare parts; working on electronics; peering through microscopes or at flickering computer screens. When she looked at their faces, they were as expressionless as dolls.

Nobody looked at her. Nobody challenged her. She felt invisible. She moved among them with greater confidence trying to find her bearings.

She checked her computerised layout.

The core to Sector D was on the hundredth level. It was there she would find the personnel computer which held Sasha's file. She took a lift, ascending swiftly up and up through the glassy building, until the people below diminished to specks. No one in the lift took any notice of her. No one it seemed was programmed to observe strangers.

The lift took an hour to reach level 100. Devi was alone by the time it arrived. When the doors slid open, she stepped out on to a smooth metal floor, ideally suited for the movement of artificial limbs. The directions turned her south and then east. Suddenly, she came to a pronged bridge which, like the spokes of a wheel, led to the hub where the personnel computer gleamed and flickered.

Devi checked her watch. Her time had already run out. To go on would mean being late returning to her sector and she would surely be discovered. Yet, if she turned back now, she would never find Sasha.

She crossed the bridge. Below her, a chasm of a hundred floors dropped away. People scurried about like ants – barely discernible. Shuddering with vertigo, she averted her eyes and hurried to the control centre.

Devi took her place in front of the vast computer and urgently began to hammer out all Sasha's details. She could be stopped at any moment. Columns of facts reeled before her eyes. Devi longed to linger over Sasha's life history, for so much of it was hers too, but she hurried on through the files – year after year – until she came to this year, when the brain scanner had detected mind pictures in Sasha's memory lobe area.

Devi read the final lines of Sasha's file:

Trial period: failure
Decommissioning
confirmed for Thursday
10, Ipsylon month, 5040
Location: Swift Hill Farm

Devi checked her watch, but she knew

with dreadful certainty that the tenth was
the next day. She had one day to find Swift
Hill Farm.

6 Outside and beyond

TODAY WAS LIKE the last day on earth. Devi felt as if she were floating disembodied. Soon she would no longer be part of the Dome. There was no turning back now. On this day – her last – she had only one thought and that was to find Sasha.

An alarm light began flashing across the sector floor. It was accompanied by a siren and a voice calling, 'Emergency! Emergency!'

The clone workers stopped and automatically moved into evacuation procedures.

Devi felt all her senses and powers concentrate into one single thought. The sirens were for her. Someone had betrayed her.

Swift Hill Farm had been designed on the old model of the outside world. Instead of glass, metal and gleaming smooth materials to help the free movement of artificial limbs, it used old world images – organic life forms. There were trees, flowers, grass, certain kinds of pre-Dome animals which had died out long ago, like cows, sheep and pigs. There was land, water and sky. Things which she had begun to see through her mind pictures. Swift Hill Farm was where they returned you to the natural world. This was decommissioning. Death.

Swift Hill . . . Swift Hill . . . Devi tried to think calmly. She had to find a route there. The siren wailed behind her. Quick, quick, her brain urged her. She tapped away furiously. It was top secret. There must be one word which would access it. She made a list of all the images she had seen at Swift Hill Farm – animal, vegetable and mineral – and asked the computer for a word which described it all. The computer flashed and stalled. It had been programmed not to answer such a question. But Devi persisted. She must trick the computer. She tried again. 'What is in or by or from something inevitable? What is the cause of everything?'

The computer beeped uncomfortably, then produced one word which flickered

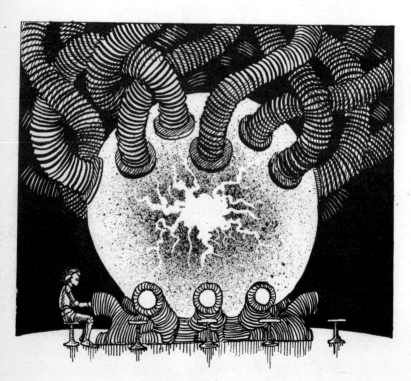

briefly on the screen before vanishing.

Nature

'Nature!' Devi tapped it out and demanded clarification. It came:

The physical power which causes the phenomena of the material world

Swift Hill Farm was the outside world. Sasha was already outside the Dome!

The alarm sirens were a continuous shriek now. Brain guardians had been summoned. The whole Dome was on alert for her.

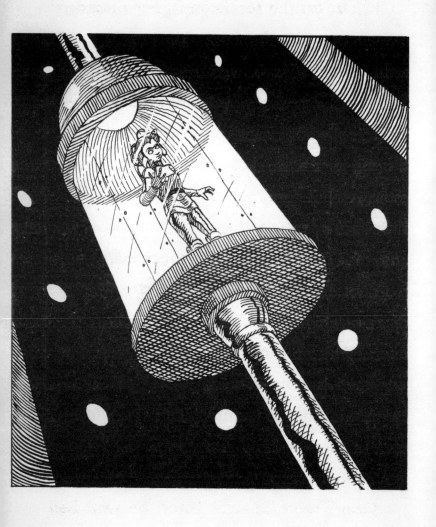

The first lift had brought her a hundred floors upwards, now she found herself before another lift which would take her up a further hundred floors. She stopped thinking. This was beyond her comprehension. She was in a dark vertical tunnel of a lift shaft, shooting upwards like a comet in space.

Above her suddenly appeared a small square of pale light. 'This is the sky.' She said the words out loud and trembled with wonder. This was the real sky. She had never before seen the sky.

A voice was shouting in her artificial sound enhancers. 'Devi! Come back!' She wanted to ignore it, but it was the Tutor. Dear Tutor; beloved Tutor; he who had been everything to her. She longed to turn back to him. She hesitated. Her eyes hurt with the almost unbearable light. With halting steps she went outside. Painfully, she saw a high green hill, its horizons curving away as if it were a planet on top of another planet. Its contours merged with the bright blue sky and then fell to somewhere below. As she stood she could hear a sound which gathered and rose louder and louder, then crashed and fell away, dwindling only to repeat the sound again and again like a recurring song. It sent shivers of memory slithering through her brain.

She tried to walk, but the surface was alien to her limbs. She tumbled and rolled,

her body clattering and screeching against
the rocks and stones.

She picked herself up and stood
wonderingly. A bird flew on to her
shoulder, hammered her curiously with its

beak and flew off. A cow came up and
nuzzled her hard limbs with its great soft
nose. A wind rippled through the long
grass. Its breath didn't penetrate her
metallic skin, but she felt its coldness on
the surface of her eyes.

She blinked. Then she saw Sasha standing in the middle of long grass, looking discarded and abandoned. They had stripped away her metallic coating and she stood raw, pale-earth-coloured, biodegradable in nature.

'Sasha!'

Sasha turned. Such joy radiated from her as she saw Devi. She ran towards her. Her dancer's body moved easily without its metal coating – as if designed for this kind of place. She reached Devi and wound her arms round her.

'I knew you would come,' she whispered.

A soft whirring sound mingled with the wind. It was the lift.

'Devi!' Raan stood with his arms outstretched towards her. 'Devi! Don't go.' He tried to move towards her.

'Raan?' Disappointment swept over her as she saw the brain guardians behind him. It must have been Raan who reported her.

'Go back, Raan. We aren't friends any more.'

'Devi!' his voice called out desperately. 'I have come to help you?'

'Why have you come with the brain guardians? You betrayed me.'

'I didn't, Devi! I swear. I came to warn you but they were here already.'

Then a razor-sharp pain seared through Devi's head, bringing her to an instant standstill. Another voice reverberated around her brain. 'Devi, come back! This is your tutor. Hear me! Listen to me! It is not time for you to be decommissioned. Return to the Dome. You still have a chance. This act of treason will be overlooked if you return now. Everything you see is an illusion!'

The Tutor's voice enticed her softly now, persuasively. 'Nothing exists outside the Dome, believe me. This is just a simulated holding place for the decommissioned. Come back, I beg you.'

Devi fancied she heard tears of anguish in the voice. She turned, listening. The Tutor's voice continued soft and enticing. 'The outside world was destroyed. It cannot support life of any kind. Come back into the safe haven. This is where you belong. Come back and be my successor so that I may at last die. Please.' His voice nearly broke up with pleading. 'I do not want to live for ever.'

Then she knew it wasn't Raan who had

betrayed her. She looked at her friend with great love. 'Go back, Raan. There's no need for you to die. Go back. I understand everything now. You were always my friend.'

The brain guardians moved forward menacingly. They emitted a soft piercing signal to immobilise her brain. Devi could hear it throbbing into all the regions of her mind. She felt her limbs beginning to weaken. And all the time, the Tutor's voice pleaded and reasoned and persuaded.

'I . . . I . . .' Devi stammered. 'I only wanted . . . to know . . . whether . . . is there a future for me and my sister outside the Dome?'

'There is no life outside the Dome – believe me,' the Tutor's voice whispered hypnotically. 'But you can live, if you return.'

. 'I will never leave my sister,' wept Devi. She turned away.

Sasha picked up two rocks and smashed them over Devi's ears. Her artificial sound enhancers cracked like the crust of a crab. Now she was deaf to the sound of the Dome.

'There *is* life outside the Dome. *This* is life. Swift Hill Farm is real,' Sasha shouted.

'There's no going back, is there?' Devi whispered.

'No,' answered Sasha.

Wrapping their arms round each other,

Devi and Sasha ran and tripped and
tumbled down the long green slope,
nearer and nearer to the sound which
gathered and rose and crashed and
dwindled away.

They reached the edge and rolled over into space. They were falling a long way down. Devi thought she heard Raan's far way voice . . . far, far away in the distance . . . his long cry of despair.

A great arc of grey; a shining surface rising and falling, sometimes grey or blue or green; a great, white wall towering sheer and high into the ever expanding blue light; and living creatures flying, swooping, diving and calling.

Among the shattered fragments of her metallic skin and artificial limbs, Devi lay on her back a long time, half in and half out of the sea. Her eyes took in a grey pebble beach which curved away in a wide arc and, rising up and up, brilliantly

white towering cliffs, from which the gulls

swooped and screeched.

Mind pictures. Devi remembered.

Hundred of years ago, there was a time when her ancestor had been a child who played on a pebble beach and lived outside the Dome. The memory genes had passed on through one generation to another until they reached Devi – and they had been revived during her brain boost. Memories from a long, long time ago. Memories forbidden in the Dome.

'We won't ever . . .' Sasha's voice whispered in her head, 'ever be parted again . . .'

A wave lapped into her face. Devi turned to her sister and stretched out a hand. She had never been aware of touch before. Skin on skin; their fingers curled

into each others as their senses faded.

'Never.'

They heard children running, tense with curiosity. 'Look what we've found!'

Faces bent over them; sweet breath filled their nostrils; fingers explored and probed; voices wondered what they were.

The Tutor had lied. There had always been life outside.

'I know now what we could have been,' breathed Devi, as the sea rolled them over and over.

If you enjoyed this
MAMMOTH READ try:

Someone's Watching, Someone's Waiting

Jamila Gavin
Illustrated by *Anthony Lewis*

What is the secret of Cote's Hall?

Emma is bored staying at Cote's Hall
until she discovers a beautiful doll in
Granny Easter's room. From that
moment, her quiet holiday becomes a
chilling nightmare . . .

A mysterious figure waves
from a window . . .

A restless voice calls her name over
and over again . . .

Then Emma discovers the awful
history of the large old house . . .

A shocking ghost story which
chills to the bone.

If you enjoyed this
MAMMOTH READ try:

Carly's Luck

Rachel Anderson
Illustrated by *Harmen Van Straaten*

Carly can look after herself.
She likes it on her own and she
doesn't need friends.
She definitely doesn't need foster
parents – even if her mum
is in hospital.

But Mr and Mrs Bear show her
kindness and warmth – no matter
how badly she behaves.

Perhaps it's nice to have friends
after all . . .

If you enjoyed this
MAMMOTH READ try:

Dead Trouble

Keith Gray
Illustrated by *Clive Scruton*

What a find! It was lying there –
just like the ones real cowboys use.

Sean and Jarrod hide the deadly
prize in their den.

Then Old Man Cooney discovers
their secret . . .

A heart-pounding adventure.

If you enjoyed this
MAMMOTH READ try:

The Stare

Pat Moon
Illustrated by *Greg Gormley*

Jenna can't believe it – just by staring
at someone she can make them do
whatever she likes! The results are
hilarious – not to mention chaotic!

Her best friend, Eddie, thinks it's
the most amazing gift – Jenna really
is telepathic. Then he discovers
the secret behind Jenna's
new-found talent.

But when he tries to warn her, she
just won't listen . . .

If you enjoyed this
MAMMOTH READ try:

Secret Friend

Pete Johnson
Illustrated by *Ken Cox*

What's worse than the first day
at a new school?
Being befriended by the most
unpopular person in the class,
that's what.

At first, Steve is grateful to Adrian.
But he soon discovers why Adrian is
so friendly: no one likes him,
especially the class bullies.

Adrian's not that bad – a bit nerdy,
perhaps, but a good mate.
How can Steve be his friend and
avoid being bullied himself?

Has Steve the courage to stand up
for Adrian, or will he always be
a secret friend?